# WILD BABIES

## SEYMOUR SIMON

 HarperCollins*Publishers*

# INTRODUCTION

Baby animals come in many sizes, shapes, and colors. You may have seen litters of kittens or puppies, but how about a lynx kitten, or a baby koala? There are more than a million kinds of animals in the world, and in this book we'll talk about some of the wild baby animals you may not have seen.

Most wild babies can move around right after they are born, and some are already able to care for themselves. But many animal mothers—such as elephants, polar bears, and giraffes—stay with their young to protect and feed them. Other mothers, such as frogs and alligators, have little or no contact with their babies. Fathers don't often play a role in raising their babies, but look to the emperor penguin for one notable exception.

In this book you'll learn where and how a variety of wild babies are born and how they live. Some are fuzzy and adorable, others are slippery or scary, but all are fascinating.

# KOALA

A koala looks very much like a toy teddy bear, but it is not a bear and isn't even related to bears. The koala is a marsupial, or pouched animal, that lives in Australia.

When a baby koala is born, it is only about as big as your little finger. Right after birth the baby crawls into its mother's pouch. There the single baby nurses and grows for six months. At that point it has all its fur and emerges from the pouch and begins to ride on its mother's back.

Koalas live among the high branches of eucalyptus trees. Eucalyptus leaves are poisonous to people and most other mammals, but koalas eat them without harm.

An adult koala is about as big as a one-year-old human, and the mother will continue to carry her baby until it is nearly as big as she is. A father koala shows no interest in the baby and even seems annoyed if a baby climbs on his back.

After four years the young koala is full-grown and moves off on its own.

# KANGAROO

Like koalas, kangaroos live in Australia and carry their young in pouches, usually just one baby per pouch. There are several different kinds of kangaroos. The great kangaroo can grow about as big as a person and weigh as much as 200 pounds. But there are also little kangaroos called wallabies that are as small as rabbits. And some kangaroos are even smaller, no bigger than rats.

A baby kangaroo is called a joey. The red kangaroo joey shown here was only about as big as a bean at birth. Like a koala baby, a joey crawls into its mother's pouch, where it nurses and grows for the first six months of its life. When it gets older, a joey sticks its head out of the pouch to see what's happening in the outside world. The joey gets a speedy ride, as its mother can hop along faster than a person can run.

Kangaroos often travel in groups or herds. A herd has no fixed home and may range over miles of Australian outback. At night they just lie down and sleep on the ground wherever they are. Many years ago herds of a thousand were not unusual, but nowadays the herds are much smaller, usually just a few dozen.

At less than a year old, the joey is grazing on plants alongside its mother and other kangaroos. Still, the joey will continue to catch rides in Mom's pouch until it is about fifteen months old.

# OPOSSUM

The Virginia opossum shown here also carries its young in a pouch—like the kangaroo and the koala. Opossums are the only marsupials in the United States, and are actually the only marsupials in the world outside of Australia, Tasmania, and New Guinea.

Unlike the koala or the kangaroo, a mother opossum gives birth to as many as fifty babies at one time, each as tiny as your thumb. Most of the babies don't live very long, though. As soon as a baby is born, it pulls itself along the mother's fur and into her pouch. The first babies attach themselves to teats and remain fastened there for about ten weeks. But the mother opossum has only thirteen teats, so the latecomers find all the feeding stations taken and do not survive.

The feeding babies grow rapidly—in only about a week they are already ten times as big as they were at birth. When the babies grow too large to fit into their mother's pouch, they hitch a ride on her back. They hang on to the mother's fur while she looks for food, such as insects, plants, and dead animals. During the time they are with their mother, young opossums learn the distinctive trick of "playing possum": They learn to roll into a tight ball and act dead at the approach of danger.

After only three or four months the babies are big enough to make their own way in the world.

# RACCOON

Raccoons are found from the southern portion of Canada through the United States and into parts of Mexico. Home is a hollow tree or a protected cave. Raccoons will eat nearly anything, including poultry, birds' eggs, insects, fish, frogs, nuts, and wild fruit.

In the spring, in April or May, a mother raccoon gives birth to four to six babies. They are covered with warm fur coats at birth but don't open their eyes until they are about three weeks old.

After another four or five weeks they will be big enough to venture out for the first time. The young raccoons walk along in single file behind their mother. Occasionally a baby will stray to look at something of interest, but then it seems to realize that it is all alone and runs to catch up with the rest of the family.

If danger comes, the mother pushes the babies up the nearest tree. Then she leads her attacker in a chase away from her children. The raccoon mother puts up a furious fight if she's cornered. When the danger is past, the mother returns to her babies and leads them back to the safety of the den.

The raccoons will stay a family for about a year, and then the babies venture off to have families of their own.

# POLAR BEAR

Polar bears live in the Arctic, along the edges of cold ocean waters. The bears are good swimmers and hunters. They catch and eat fish, seals, and walruses.

During the middle of winter, while a polar bear mother is hibernating, she gives birth to one to three cubs in a den dug out of snow and ice. The cubs are born hairless and blind, but the body heat of the mother keeps the den 40 degrees Fahrenheit warmer than the outside temperature.

Cubs weigh only about 2 pounds at birth but grow rapidly as they nurse on their mother's butterfat-rich milk. As the weeks pass, they open their eyes; soft fur covers their bodies. Polar bears have a special kind of fur that traps heat and keeps them warm.

By the spring, when the long winter sleep ends, the cubs weigh 25 pounds. Now the babies get their first look at the outside world. They slide in the snow and play-fight with each other. There is plenty of time for play as the cubs grow, because they will follow along with their mother for the next two years, slowly learning how to hunt food for themselves.

# EMPEROR PENGUIN

The female emperor penguin lays a single egg on the shores of the cold Antarctic ocean, half a world away from the polar bear but in much the same kind of icy surroundings. She lays her egg in a place called a rookery, where hundreds of thousands of other mother penguins are also laying their eggs. In the wild, being part of a large group can be very helpful. A group of penguins has thousands of eyes that keep a sharp watch on nearby waters, where leopard seals and killer whales prowl.

After she lays her egg, the mother waddles down to the sea and swims away to find food—small fish and krill, a kind of tiny shrimp—and she doesn't come back for two months! The male penguin takes care of the egg, balancing it on the tops of his wide feet and pulling down a feathery pouch from his belly to keep it warm.

When the penguin chick hatches, it is covered by downy feathers that protect it against the cold. Now the mother penguin returns, and the father can finally go back to the sea to feed—he's lost a lot of weight after not eating for two months!

For seven months the penguin chicks are kept in huge "kindergartens," where a few adults can care for many young at one time. The growing chicks spend four years learning how to swim and fish together in underwater schools. A penguin chick quickly learns how to work and play well with others.

# GIRAFFE

A newborn giraffe seems to be all long legs and neck. It's as tall as a person and weighs 150 wobbly pounds at birth. For the first few days the mother licks and noses her calf. She is cleaning it and learning its particular odor. The smell of her calf will help her locate it in the midst of a herd. Sounds also help them keep in touch, so a calf may bleat to get its mother's attention.

When they are one to two weeks old, giraffe calves join calf groups, called kindergartens. A dozen calves may be watched by two or three "baby-sitting" females. The tall giraffe adults can see dangerous lions, leopards, or wild dogs a long way off. The mothers range far afield to find the great quantities of tree leaves they need to cat each day to produce rich milk for the babies. For a month they return twice a day to the herd to feed their calves. After that the calves begin to eat leaves like adult giraffes.

Giraffes are the tallest living animals in the world. Adults can reach almost 20 feet, nearly twice as high as a basketball hoop, and weigh more than 2,000 pounds. As big and powerful as giraffes are, they are very peaceful animals. A herd of giraffes on the move can look like a bunch of giant long-stemmed flowers flowing across the African plains.

# ELEPHANT

About the only land animal that weighs much more than a giraffe is the African elephant. Even a newborn elephant calf is big. The little bundle of joy weighs more than 200 pounds but looks tiny beneath its huge mother, who weighs thirty or forty times that. The mother helps the calf to its feet by gently putting her foot under it and lifting it. She tucks the baby under her chin and strokes and steadies it with her trunk.

For the first six months the mother follows her calf everywhere, never letting it out of her sight. The baby elephant stays with its mother for at least three years and sometimes as long as eight to ten years. It watches its mother carefully and learns what foods to eat and the location of water holes and mud wallows.

Elephants travel in herds made up of females and young males; adult males travel alone. Young females in the herd will help the mothers look after and protect the calves. And at the slightest sign of danger, the entire herd will circle around a mother and her calf and begin trumpeting and making loud noises to frighten away lions or wild dogs.

# BABOON

Baboons are big African monkeys that travel together in groups, or troops, of a hundred or more. Baboons live mostly on the ground, rather than in trees as most other monkeys do. A baboon baby needs to hold on tightly to its mother so it won't fall off as the troop moves across rocky cliffs or other rough terrain.

A baby is usually cared for by its mother and two or three special friends. These are often young males who set about making friendly faces and funny noises at the baby and spend a lot of time grooming it. This is serious business for a young male baboon. If he doesn't make a good baby-sitter, he'll be ousted from the troop.

Baboon babies are safe as long as they stay with the troop. If a leopard or lion tries to hunt a young baboon, the male baboons will tear the attacker to shreds with their long teeth.

As the babies grow, they learn to eat what other baboons eat—which is almost anything: fruits, roots, insects, even small snakes. When baboons find food, they can either eat it right away or store it in pouches in their cheeks to be eaten later.

# DOLPHIN

Even though dolphins live in the sea, they are mammals, not fish, so they breathe air through lungs. A baby dolphin is born underwater, and the newborn calf must quickly get up to the surface to take its first breath of air. If the baby is too weak to swim, the mother will push it to the surface.

As soon as a baby is born, the mother and her calf begin whistling at each other. They learn to recognize each other through sounds. Dolphins have a complicated language of whistles, clicks, clacks, and squawks. If the baby wanders away, the mother need only whistle for it to come back.

Dolphins travel in communities called pods, and calves play together in a "playpen" formed by two or three females circling around them for protection. But a calf still relies on its mother; it will continue to nurse for about a year and a half.

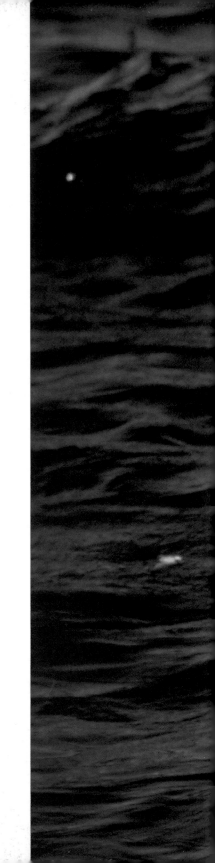

# FROG

Frogs come out of hibernation sometime between the end of March and the beginning of May. They make their way to a breeding pond, usually the one where they were hatched. Spawning begins suddenly in the pond one night, and by the next morning hundreds of frogs will have laid hundreds of thousands of eggs.

Every few seconds a female frog lays a burst of hundreds of eggs, which are immediately fertilized by a male. An egg looks like a small black bead, about the size of a pinhead. The eggs are surrounded by a clear jelly that swells up in the water and clumps the eggs together in large masses. After egg laying neither parent takes any further interest in their offspring.

Tadpoles hatch in one to three weeks, depending upon the water temperature. Each tiny tadpole struggles free of the jelly and soon swims about in search of tiny green plants called algae. The tadpoles are themselves eaten by all kinds of fish, insects, and even other frogs. The vast numbers of tadpoles that hatch help insure that some will survive to become adults.

During the next two or three months the tadpoles will change greatly. First small hind legs begin to grow, then front legs, and then the tadpoles lose their tails. These new froglets are now ready to leave the pond. Once on land they will hunt for insects and other prey. In two or three years they will return to the pond to spawn a new generation.

# ALLIGATOR

The American alligator lives in rivers and swamps in the southeastern United States, particularly in Florida. A female alligator makes a plant-and-mud nest that is more than 3 feet high and 6 feet across. She lays between twenty and forty eggs, each about the size of a chicken's egg, and then covers them with another layer of plants and mud. An alligator does not sit on her nest the way a bird does; instead, the eggs are warmed by the sun and also by the heat given off by the rotting plant materials in the nest. But she will stay nearby and protect the nest for two to three months until the eggs hatch.

When the baby alligators are ready to hatch, they make squeaking sounds from within the eggs. The mother hears the squeaks and removes the top layer of the nest. A baby alligator rips through its leathery white shell with an egg tooth, a horny growth on the tip of its snout. The mother stays with her babies only a short time after they hatch; then they are on their own.

Newborn alligators are about 8 to 10 inches long. The young are hunted by many animals, including fish, birds, and larger alligators. Thousands are also sold as pets or stuffed souvenirs. A baby grows quickly—about a foot a year for the first three or four years. An average adult is 6 to 8 feet, though some may grow to twice that size.

# LYNX

The Canadian lynx lives in the forests of Canada and as far south as Oregon and Colorado in the west and northern New York state in the east. An adult is 3 feet long, as large as a medium-sized dog.

A litter of about four lynx kittens is born in early spring, usually in the shelter of an overhanging rock or in a thicket of trees. Like domestic kittens, they are blind at birth and won't open their eyes for about ten days. The mother lynx nurses them for two or three months. Then the kittens are old enough to travel with their mother when she goes hunting for snowshoe rabbits, small birds, and rodents. The lynx often hunts at night. It has such good eyes that sharp-sighted people are sometimes called "lynx eyed."

By midsummer the kittens are independent and hunting for themselves. But they still may stay together until the winter, when they are full-grown.

photo credits: jacket, © Marshall Sklar/Photo Researchers, Inc.; pp. 1, 22, 29, © Stan Osolinski/Dembinsky Photo Association; pp. 2–3, 14–15, © Dan Guravich/Photo Researchers, Inc.; pp. 4, 30, © Alan D. Carey/Photo Researchers, Inc.; pp. 7, 8, © Tom McHugh/Photo Researchers, Inc.; p. 11, © Yeager & Kay/Photo Researchers, Inc.; p. 12, © Jeanne White/Photo Researchers, Inc.; p. 17 © Mark J. Thomas/Dembinsky Photo Association; p. 18, © Gregory G. Dimijian/Photo Researchers, Inc.; pp. 20–21, © Tim Davis/Photo Researchers, Inc.; pp. 24–25, © Peter Howorth/Mo Yung Productions; p. 26, © Nuridsany et Pérennou/Photo Researchers, Inc.; p. 32, © Sandved Photography/Photo

Library of Congress Cataloging-in-Publication Data
Simon, Seymour.
  Wild babies / by Seymour Simon.
    p.    cm.
  Summary: Describes the various parenting techniques of different types of wild animals and provides a close look at the behavior and characteristics of their offspring.
    ISBN 0-06-023033-9. — ISBN 0-06-023034-7 (lib. bdg.) — ISBN 0-06-446206-4 (pbk.)
    1. Animals—Infancy—Juvenile literature.   2. Parental behavior in animals—Juvenile literature.   [1. Animals—Infancy.   2. Parental behavior in animals.]   I. Title.
QL763.S535    1997                                                                96-14558
591.3'9—dc20                                                                      CIP
                                                                                 AC

Typography by Al Cetta ❖ Visit us on the World Wide Web! http://www.harperchildrens.com